I0530920

THE WORLD WHERE LOVE

NEVER DIES

PRELUDE

By

Jean Vincent Naurais

Copyright © 2020 Jean Vincent Naurais

ISBN: 978-1-7358113-6-9 (Paperback)

Library of Congress Control Number: 2020920886

Front cover: Painting by Artist Marianne Nems

www.MarianneNems.com

Book design by JV Naurais

Copy editing: Francisco Rodriguez & Michael Lutz

Printed by Amazon KDP

First printing edition 2020

Publisher: Lips to Ears

1000 5th street suite 200T4

Miami Beach, FL, 33139 USA

www.Naurais.com

PREFACE

This series of books is dedicated to the Readers who will confidently change their life because of it. Every word has been written with this mission in mind, divinely infused one night, when life felt hopeless. I have been told to write it and it took me a lifetime effort to achieve it.

This body of work uses a language by its own, deeply rooted in its structure, a language who will eventually speak to your soul. It is a language that is not made to run through your brain. It is not a language that you have to define. Chapters are written as a trilogy, the rhythms of these are all appropriate. You will discover why any deep message, at any given time, has to be delivered three times. You will certainly discover why it always begins chapter 0, as the perfection of nothingness, and ends a cycle chapter 21, three times. There is no coincidence here. No need to struggle to understand now. When the time is right, you will.

The emerging element of understanding will jump up, hopefully changing your own life too, all over again... And that will be our success, you as the reader and me as the author.

I believe in this: When we change the way we look at things, things we look at change. I am already starting , changing the way to look at dedication and acknowledgment. This is the reason why there is above all, only one dedication and acknowledgment I wanted to proclaim loud and clear: These books are dedicated to YOU.

PRELUDE

The power of now! Right, I am just surviving. I think I want to grow rich, yet even if I read these books a hundred times I am still going to be in the same situation and broke on top of that. I need romance, I need the right alchemist to show me the way. I am a free spirit and so I ask my dear God if by any chance He could intervene? I am not here in this life for nothing!

Despite my positive thinking, as you can see, I cannot

find my way! I have read a few spiritual books which I believe I did not understand. Do I need to search for more? I need to find meaning here and now.

Not long ago, I was thinking big. I trusted a lot of people to partner with me following my dream plan. But it did not work the way I thought it would, and I got ripped-off along the way. How can I forgive these people?

There is no magic that works when it's time to pay the bills. I really wonder how I can change all this. I want to live this enlightenment everybody's talking about —I want to be happy in that world of kindness I keep hearing about.

Of course I like kindness too, though I almost forgot it exists. And I always try to be kind myself. But I was losing this kind approach as well as my motivation in life. I still had a spark of light here and there to motivate myself, just a bit left over.

So I decided to buy self-motivation books, as many as possible. Nothing worked. This was not the journey of the soul that I was going through, but the journey of the fool... This was my journey! As my ex-girlfriend told me:

"You need a love story in your life... but... not with me."

I think she was right up to but, really?

I was supposed to be a writer writing, but I was spending more time thinking "why should I follow my dream if it does not work?" than making it real. You may know what I am talking about...

There are many writers in the world: the ones that write blogs, the ones that do whatever as long as it is writing; then there is real journalism writing; and people who write love letters and there is me, a new species of writer, a modern twist, "a-wonder-of-you" writer...

Maybe I should change careers and become a tattoo artist, at least I would then write the bare minimum, get it? And it would stay written for a lifetime.

This is the plan. I need to interview some tattoo artists. I saw this reality TV show about tattoo artists. I can write about their feelings when they tattoo words, knowing that their work will eternally stay, I mean, until they die, and if they are not cremated, of course.

My boss, because I have a boss too; my boss is

harassing me, asking me twice a day when will I be able to produce an article for the divine blog he is managing. If he keeps this up I will give him my story on how to peel potatoes without using your hands.

The boss:

"Hey, are you sleeping? Stop dreaming, time to work. Wake up! What's your next topic?"

The journalist:

OMG, my boss is keeping me from getting some sleep here! What I'm going to say to him... "Well, yes, no, I'm sorry. I am scheduling some interviews with tattoo artists in LA."

The boss:

"What's her name?"

The journalist, hesitating:

"Well... Alexia!"

The boss:

"The one from the reality TV show?"

The journalist:

"Yes, I will interview her about what people ask her

to write on their bodies. It's just an idea I need to develop."

The boss:

"Well, it seems interesting."

The journalist, thinking:

Oh boy. I had just come up with her name from the TV show when he woke me up. So I guess I need to call her now.

The next day I was at her shop like thirty minutes before opening, as agreed. She was not there yet. Next door was this man who looked homeless in front of a shop with a sign in big letters "Astrology & Psychotherapist."

The homeless man:

"Do you want me to do your tarots?"

The journalist:

"Now? How long does it take?"

The homeless/tarot reader:

"About five minutes for five dollars. If you like, it will be fifty dollars for thirty minutes."

The journalist:

"OK, let's do it. But just for five, I am waiting for Alexia, your neighbor. Do you know her?"

The homeless/tarot reader:

"OK please sit here, I can start quickly (pulling a few cards...) Nothing is going to be the same for you. You have a new lover coming into your life, it is like news coming. She will be announced, or will announce news... I hope you are ready for this..."

The journalist:

"What do you mean? Do I need to prepare myself? What do I need to do?"

The homeless/tarot reader:

"Let me see, no, someone will prepare you for it. Like a figure, maybe a father-figure for you, the Emperor."

The journalist:

"Do you mean I need to ask my Dad to help me? To be clean maybe? No, you are joking, an Emperor?"

The homeless/tarot reader:

"Clean in your mind, yes. The Emperor is the card!

Your new love will be a passion. That is for sure."

The journalist:

"Well, do you see her number by any chance? How does she look?"

The homeless/tarot reader:

"Don't, I need to focus, you have a kind of synchronicity here, I mean, growth, spiritually speaking. There will be important news for you. Someone is going to bring you messages.

You have chosen a new direction. It's coming.

You have the Wheel of Fortune. It's a consistent message for you today. This is great. You need to pay attention.

We have the Queen of Cups in your challenge, and the Emperor is advice from spirits, and the Five of Wands for the outcome.

Hey, you have the Fool too. That's it, if you want more it will be an additional $45."

The journalist:

"You speak a language I don't know. Is it what I am

thinking? I was beginning to think that I was the Fool in this life, is this my journey? It does not matter; I think I just started it.

Here you go $50, give me back the five, but I have my appointment coming up so can we finish right after it?"

The homeless/tarot reader:

"Not really, it comes as a full package, cannot be disrupted. And later I need to be somewhere else."

The journalist:

"OK, OK, so what's next, what will happen to me?"

The homeless/tarot reader:

"Let me pull more cards... I need to clarify...

I love this energy, the Ace of Swords. Please spirits, give us your advice...

The King of Wands, Leo Energy, covered by the High Priestess... represents a master and someone who understands how to use energy to his advantage, a good leader, knows how to bring success to life, humm... by lifting the veil on the spiritual...

The journalist:

"That sounds good? I always feel like a king, deep inside."

The homeless/tarot reader:

"Yes it is you, the Emperor is the man, father-figure. He is going to make you do... things...

You will trust your intuition; follow what your intuition maybe... is telling you. You need to look at something in a different way. That will happen with his help, the Emperor's.

You will have different opportunities... that will open up for you. It also looks like you had it already not knowing it... or not knowing how to use what you have...

All this will bring success into your life. You will take your power back moving in that direction. You will know you will have to move forward. You will have to take charge in order to bring success into your life. You will have a moment of clarity. After that, your great success will come along."

The journalist:

"Clarity? Like Enlightenment?"

The homeless/tarot reader:

"Absolutely... Oh my God, you also have the two and the eight, so the total is ten. It's also the number of the Wheel of Fortune. I can see, you want it so much... it will happen. It is confirmed.

Let me see here...

This is interesting, you have the Queen of Cups here... In your challenge, you also have the Page of Swords... you may have bad news, and it is brought to you, or you get it, and it's linked to your relationship, so you will need to do something, to get your Queen...

Things will shift in your favor. But you will need to trust your intuition even if you get bad news, just go for it; take your chances.

Again, I see you have the Nine of Swords, it means news, conversations. I see some good news or good conversations...

No, but I see bad news, a link to your destiny... Okay, I get it, some good, for a new beginning and perseverance through bad news...

It will be a sudden change; you will just know when it happens.

You have this energy that will grow, like energy of faith, but not blind faith. Instead, you will see and will have faith.

That's it. Do you have any questions?"

The journalist:

"When will this happen?"

The homeless/tarot reader:

"In that order, you have already started. Okay, thank you. I need to leave this place."

The journalist:

"I can see Alexia has arrived, I believe she is opening the door of her shop, so thank you to you. I am very pleased. I also need to get going."

"Hello Alexia, how are you?"

Alexia:

"Great thank you, please come in."

The journalist:

"You have a great shop, on the show it looks smaller, but it's huge!"

Alexia:

"Yes, everybody is telling me that. What were you doing next door, are you going to interview him?"

The journalist:

"Not at all, I was waiting for you and he proposed to do my tarots."

Alexia:

"Really, that guy you were with did your tarots?"

The journalist:

"Yea, why?"

Alexia:

"Because he is not the owner of that shop. I think he lives around here, he has nothing to do with the astrologist."

The journalist:

"Really?"

Alexia:

"Yes, he is kind of homeless around here. I guess he asked him to take care of his shop, he needed to pick up something for lunch."

The journalist:

"You think so?"

Alexia:

"Yea, he does that. The owner is a real psychotherapist, he is a very cool guy but kind of clean on himself, he does not look like the homeless!"

The journalist:

"OMG, you think the homeless that did my tarots is fake? Now I understand why he was in such a hurry to get my money and go!"

Alexia:

"Because, you paid him?"

The journalist:

"Yes I did, and worst; I believed everything he told me!"

Alexia:

"Haa, you are a funny guy. Hey, don't mix up my

interview with someone else's."

The journalist:

"No, don't worry. But I am so confused; he really told me things I liked."

Alexia:

"Of course, ha ha, you have these people who know how to say exactly what you want to hear and they do it so well that you are happy to pay them, ha ha..."

The journalist:

"No, but this guy, I mean, in my opinion he was gifted!"

Alexia:

"Seriously? Did he say something about me?"

The journalist:

"Not at all, it was all about me and success, love and everything... I loved it."

Alexia:

"Ha! Maybe I should ask him for a reading then. How much did he take?"

The journalist:

"Fifty bucks."

Alexia

"Fifty bucks!!! Ha... you are crazy, he is good!"

The journalist:

"Let me see if he is still here..." "Hello, hello?"

The owner of the shop:

"Yes, may I help you?"

The journalist:

"I came here a few minutes ago and met with another gentleman, gray hair. He was smoking a cigarette outside..."

The owner of the shop:

"Yes, Gary! He was just watching my store; I was getting my lunch a block away."

The journalist:

"Really, so maybe I will come back for a reading, I am with Alexia for another thirty minutes."

The owner of the shop:

"I don't do readings, I do astrology, birth charts and psychotherapy."

The journalist:

"Really? You don't do tarots?"

The owner of the shop:

"Nope."

The journalist:

"All right, I will be back anyway. Thank you."

...

"Alexia, you were right. My tarot reader was the homeless guy. I cannot believe what happened!"

Alexia:

"You know that guy, the owner, he has a great story that you may be interested in."

The journalist:

"Like what?"

Alexia:

"He had a dreadful car accident years ago. He lost his wife in that accident. He stayed in a coma for a week or something like that. He died in his hospital bed, he flat-lined. He has quite a story, super interesting. You should listen to his story."

The journalist:

"I will ask him, when was it?"

Alexia:

"Years ago I guess, when he decided to change careers. Now he is remarried."

The journalist:

"I will ask him after I am done with you. That's a great idea."

Alexia:

"So what did you want to ask me exactly?"

The journalist:

"I wanted to ask you about the texts you tattoo on people. What do they ask for? Do you have any favorite stories, short stories? I am also interested in your feelings when you are doing your thing."

After an hour of interesting anecdotes, I was ready to go back to my office to work on her interview. But before that I wanted to stop by the shop next door.

I checked what kind of shop was on the other side, just out of curiosity, in any case I would have another inspirational adventure. It was a pet shop, which did not inspire me at all.

I was already obsessed with what the homeless guy had told me and wanted to know more but him but he was gone.

And what about the real owner's story? I wanted to meet him, almost as if I was expecting him to confirm the message of the homeless man. Of course it did not happen.

As a matter of fact, I didn't even want to mention I had paid the homeless guy $50 for a reading. I did not want my messenger to get into any trouble, as I really thought he was great. I was convinced that he had not made up anything, that his message had been for me. I prayed that that message was specifically for me, no matter the source, and I wanted it to be true.

The astrologist was available for my interview so I could do it straight away.

When his accident happened, he thought: This is how we're gonna die! He had had time to think and look at the eyes of the two people in the other car they crashed into. This was his last impression when they were two feet away, the last time he saw them. He felt his wife ejecting instantly, ending up far away from the car smashing through the windshield: and then, nothing.

The next thing he knew he was rising above the scene and was next to his wife and the two people. Everybody was okay but confused. Because he knew he had to go back, he knew (and everybody knew) that he was the only one to have that possibility, and he could see his future.

He did not perceive it as an opportunity, just a possibility that would be less pleasant than to stay with them. He had a new intimate knowledge about these two people and anybody he would look at, when he was, I would say, above, for example the paramedics.

He was telling me about the connection among all mankind that religions talk about is real and so incredibly intimate.

He could say goodbye to his wife, by thought, and right after that, he was in the hospital levitating above his bed. Ever since that day he could see what he had to do on earth. He could visualize his new career. He fell in love again, and married again.

Personally I thought that was part of my own message, new career, my new love.

He called it a Near-Death Experience. He discovered he could still communicate with his past wife. When it was time, she asked him to move on with his life, when he got feelings for another woman years after the accident. It was the last time he could communicate with her, as if she was waiting for that moment to really let go.

My beliefs were up and down with this homeless man's reading and this guy's near-death experience. After all, maybe he was right, I could feel shifting already. I was hoping the bad news I would get would not be a car accident. He said: 'a new beginning and perseverance despite bad news.'

I did not care much about the interview with the tattoo girl. I did not think she would be my wife anyway, so I was still in my world of confusion and self-searching.

I was professionally... lost, like wasted. I was a specialist in this stage of confusion, where I could navigate like a real pro, because I was so used to it!

Of course when I arrived at my office my boss asked me to stop by his office. You know, like the chief of the police in movies who needs to unload his frustrations on his best agent.

He was older than me. He could have been a very young father to me, if he had been a teenage father, and nothing I would have missed out on, genetically speaking. So, he could not be the father-figure the homeless man was speaking about.

Despite the many thoughts swirling around my mind I had to listen to what he had to say. After all, it was my day to listen, I even listened to the homeless guy today for $50 bucks. At least with my boss I would be the one who got paid!

The boss:

"Listen, you need to wake up and smell the coffee! I am sure you are aware about the situation. It's time to realize and accept the truth. You are not going to work here next month unless you start, and I repeat start, working harder!"

The journalist:

"I have good news, I will survive, gain prominence and fame: And this, very soon."

The boss:

"What are you talking about? I want to see that. Please be my guess. By the way, how did you learn that?"

The journalist:

"A famous astrologist, his partner to be precise, told me."

The boss:

"And you believe him? Hum, please do, you will need it!"

The journalist:

"And I will find the love of my life. She will be announced or announcing news or something like that."

The boss:

"She is on the news? On our floor?"

The journalist:

"No boss, I don't know if she is working here, but something will happen."

The boss:

"I see. You are hiding something from me! I don't want to see you in the photocopy room hanging around!"

The journalist:

"Because you think I could find out who she is in the copy room?"

The boss:

"Get out of my office."

I kind of love my boss, he is a mess himself, it's a love-hate relationship between Monday morning and Friday at 5 pm.

When he feels like hell he wants to make everybody feel the same. He worked in the army for a few years. I guess it is like a tattoo, it's difficult to remove its imprint...

That same day I had my story done about the tattoo girl.

Now, I was free to focus on her neighbor and the homeless guy's prophecies. I had some parts of it come to mind. I tried to see if they were following some kind of logic.

This guy did overcome adversity. He had to die! That cannot be a solution. Who could be this father figure I need to meet? So, I decided to do a list of all the people I wanted to meet: male and older than me, with a certain knowledge, a father figure he had said...

Then I was searching and searching... After a few days of searching I realized I had to contact an author I had wanted to interview years ago. So I would need to stop momentarily to look for the Emperor father figure.

It could not be that author because I did not know him and had not even read any of his books. But I wanted to know him for some other reason that I still didn't know about.

I was sincerely exhausted about looking for the Emperor himself. I just wanted to take a break. I would be able to continue after my real work was done. That was what I was thinking!

A few days down the road I started to feel stupid for trying to follow the homeless guy's guidance. And what if he just wanted to get my money? $50 bucks is a fortune if you are homeless! I should have asked him about my past, it's easier and much faster to verify, at least. What I was thinking?

This author I wanted to schedule an interview with, would be like the tattoo girl. I would be in and out, same day, my boss will have his story the day after and that would be that.

Sometimes, to make a living writing, you just need to be fast and efficient. If I start to wonder and dream and fall asleep to be woken up by my boss, as happens so often, I would be that person I don't want to be. I needed motivation, I needed action, I needed results, a new life!

How can my dreams become reality when even the dreams are confused?

Thank God I did not have any hardship to overcome, like this guy who died. Or maybe this is why I am like this... I should have asked the homeless guy if I would die soon or needed to go through hardships myself. I don't know, but I am going to ask someone who knows, and someone other than Google... The Emperor.

How am I going to find the right person? I will need a miracle! And the right person to love? And who will love me? My Queen, It's a lot to unpack!

I spent a few days trying to get a hold of the phone number of this author. When I called, I got his people telling me to call back a few days later.

When I called back, to my surprise, they said he would have to call me back himself, he had insisted. With my legendary luck, how many phone calls do I need to do to get one short interview?

About a week later he called me and left a message on my answer machine. Of course, I was taking a shower when he called. I tried to call him back a few times, without success. A few days later he called me back, this time I picked up:

The old man:

"Good morning, I heard you wanted to interview me?"

The journalist:

"Good morning, how are you? Yes I do, I left all the questions I wanted to ask you with your staff. Were they alright? They asked me for them. Anyway, this does not need to be recorded and they are simple questions like how did you get started... Things like that. Your motivations in life..."

The old man:

"I see. I don't need to know. I did not read your questions. I will welcome you in three weeks. Like the trinity."

The journalist:

"I beg your pardon?"

The old man:

"Have you heard about the trinity?"

The journalist:

"From the Bible?"

The old man:

"I know You received protection, guidance and help from divine forces... I know You received protection, guidance and help from divine forces... I know You received protection, guidance and help from divine forces."

The journalist thinking:

Why did he repeat it three times? I heard it the first time. "Hello, hello, hello can you hear me now?"

The old man:

"You are going to be introduced to a new world you don't know yet, 'the world where LOVE NEVER DIES.'

I will welcome you in three weeks. Have a good day."

The journalist:

I hope he was the author. I did not have time to verify his identity, after all I have no idea if it was him. Also he hung up so fast that I did not say goodbye.

When I thought back about the homeless guy I remembered he said I would be helped. My shift has already started, he said...

Maybe the homeless guy's reading was the guidance this author was talking about when he said 'you received guidance...' and divine forces are going to help me? What the heck is that? How could he know I need help, first of all? This is too weird to be a coincidence.

I honestly thought at this point that I was trying to fit the reality to what I wanted: to match the message of the homeless guy. And why did he repeat it three times anyway, this was really weird, an enigma, or had it been a bad phone connection?

Exactly three weeks later, I was in my car arriving at his house, on time, and ready to finally understand what he was trying to tell me. Eventually ready to make a great, fast interview, that I could finish hopefully the same day, and uploaded before the end of the day to my boss, like clockwork.

Do you want to read more?

This is a Novel based on a true story.

How can you change your life? This time for sure!

Hardships, depression, anxiety, oppressive fatigue and/or physical illness may eventually and unfairly lead you into a purposeless life. But this book will change your life.

Its fundamental esoteric and spiritual teachings, thinly disguised as a novel, will become the basis for your new understanding of the Age of Aquarius.

A journalist reflects upon his long-standing need to interview a particular mystical old man, very well-known for his faithful soul and for his writings.

When they finally meet, he learns about the old man's fascinating story coming to realize how astonishingly his own life is also going to become spiritually guided in the same fashion, receiving multiple prophecies that point to a new beginning.

The life of this old man, his explanations, his teachings, sway the journalist to rethink his own values and beliefs. "We don't see things as they are, we see things as we are." Through a kind of osmosis he changes to perceive his life with a new perspective.

The old man captivates him with his story carrying him into a much higher spiritual understanding where, at last, he profoundly understands why they are meeting, and the extraordinary meaning of this "world where love never dies."

The old man and his wife lived a lush life. Early in their journey, both much younger, they did not really know where they were going. They seemed to have it all, they could do anything they wanted; they were young and foolish, pure and innocent.

They were warned of a sudden change drawing closer: a major and inexorable change, when all of a sudden, tragedy struck.

Curiously, through his life story, the old man is prophesying glimpses of an extraordinary love and a new worldwide career coming soon to the journalist's life, because of his newly acquired understanding.

Motivated by these teachings, the journalist's spiritual senses greatly developed his ability to discover his higher purpose in life: TRUE LOVE.

This is a love story he will never forget.

From the book series:

THE WORLD WHERE LOVE NEVER DIES

CHAPTER 0

A NEW BEGINNING

Book 1: THE PROPHECIES

Register now for special updates behind the scenes, offers and promotions.

www.Naurais.com/register

COMING NEXT:

THE WORLD WHERE LOVE NEVER DIES

Book 1: THE PROPHECIES

Book 2 EPIC ATTRIBUTES

Book 3 THE THREE OF LIFE

Book 4 LIPS TO EARS

Book 5 LOVE RESONANCE

Book 6 THE EYE OF WISDOM

www.ingramcontent.com/pod-product-compliance
Lightning Source LLC
Chambersburg PA
CBHW071226130626
46555CB00004B/1872